DRAW WILD ROBOT MASH-UPS

BY MARI BOLTE
ART BY LOIC BILLIAU

CAPSTONE PRESS
a capstone imprint

Edge Books are published by Capstone Press,
1710 Roe Crest Drive, North Mankato, Minnesota 56003
www.mycapstone.com

Library of Congress Cataloging-in-Publication Data
Names: Bolte, Mari, author.
Title: Draw wild robot mash-ups / by Mari Bolte.
Description: North Mankato, Minnesota : Edge Books, Capstone Press, 2018. |
Series: Drawing mash-ups | Includes bibliographical references and index.
| Audience: Ages 9–15. | Audience: Grades 4 to 6.
Identifiers: LCCN 2017021454 | ISBN 9781515769347 (library binding) |
ISBN 9781515769385 (ebook pdf)
Subjects: LCSH: Robots in art—Juvenile literature. |
Drawing—Technique—Juvenile literature.
Classification: LCC NC1764.8.R63 B65 2018 | DDC 741.5/356—dc23
LC record available at https://lccn.loc.gov/2017021454

Editorial Credits
Brann Garvey, designer; Kathy McColley, production specialist

Image Credits
Illustrations: Loic Billiau; Photos: Capstone Studio: Karon Dubke, 5 (all); Backgrounds and design elements: Capstone

Printed and bound in the USA.
010364F17

TABLE OF CONTENTS

READY, SET, ROBOT!

Do you have a mechanical mind? Put it to use! Combine two (or more!) crazy ideas together to create a robot mash-up that defies technology. Use the ideas in the book, and then re-mash them to make something even wilder! Challenge your friends to see who can draw the most futuristic features.

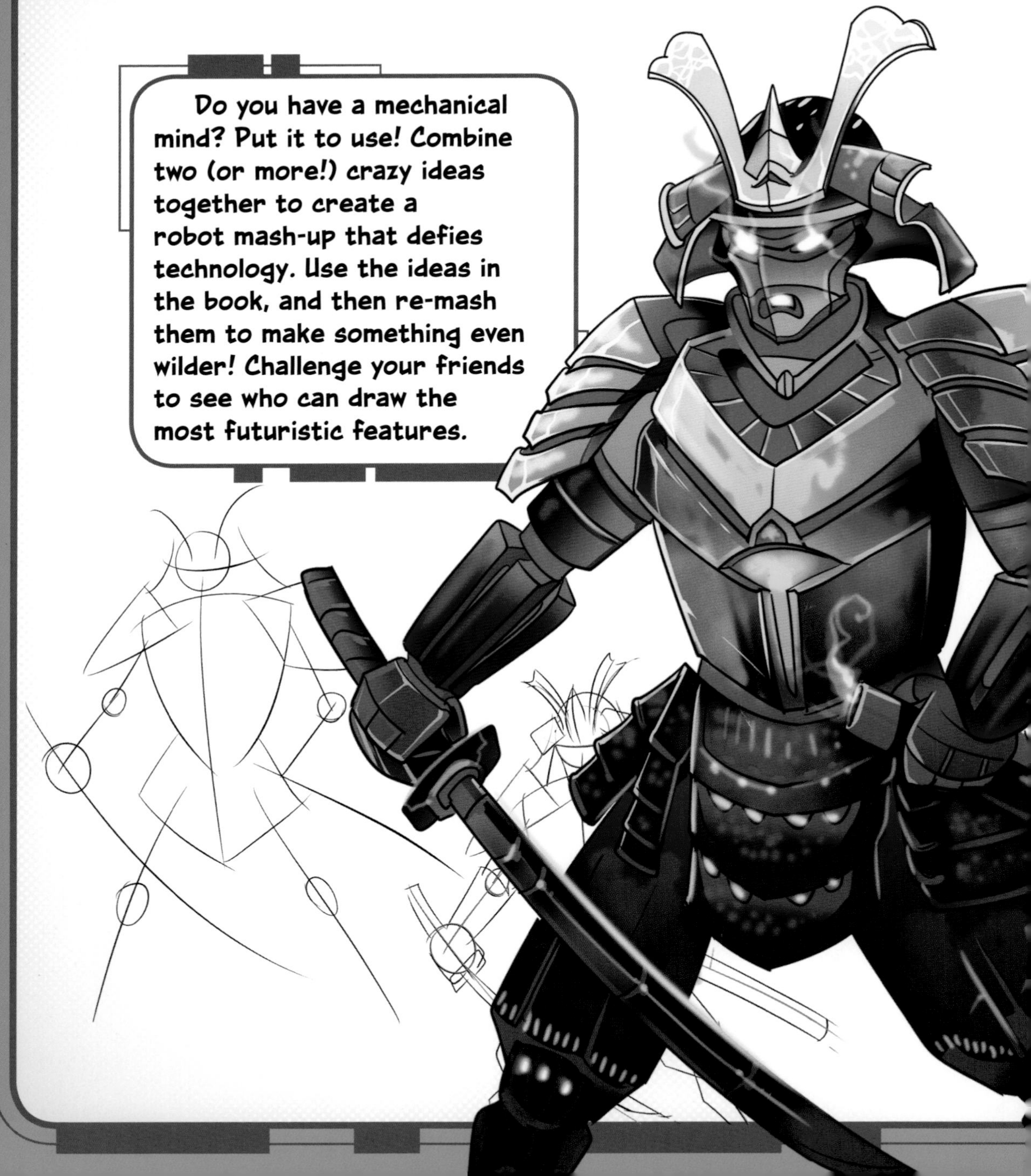

MATERIALS

The artwork in this book was created digitally, but that doesn't mean your own art can't look equally amazing.

It all starts with a pencil and paper! Use light pencil strokes to shape your creation. Shading, hatch marks, and curved lines can really make your mash-ups pop off the page.

When you're happy with how your sketches look, darken the pencil lines and erase any overlapping areas. Use a pen to outline and add shadows and detail.

Markers or colored pencils will truly bring your art to life. Experiment with shading, outlines, blending, or using different shades of the same color to make gradients. Or try out a new art supply! Chalk or watercolor pencils, oil crayons, or pastels could add an extra challenge.

RO-BOAT

What could be cooler than a boat that drives itself? This automated airboat is ready to jump from swamp to space with the touch of a button.

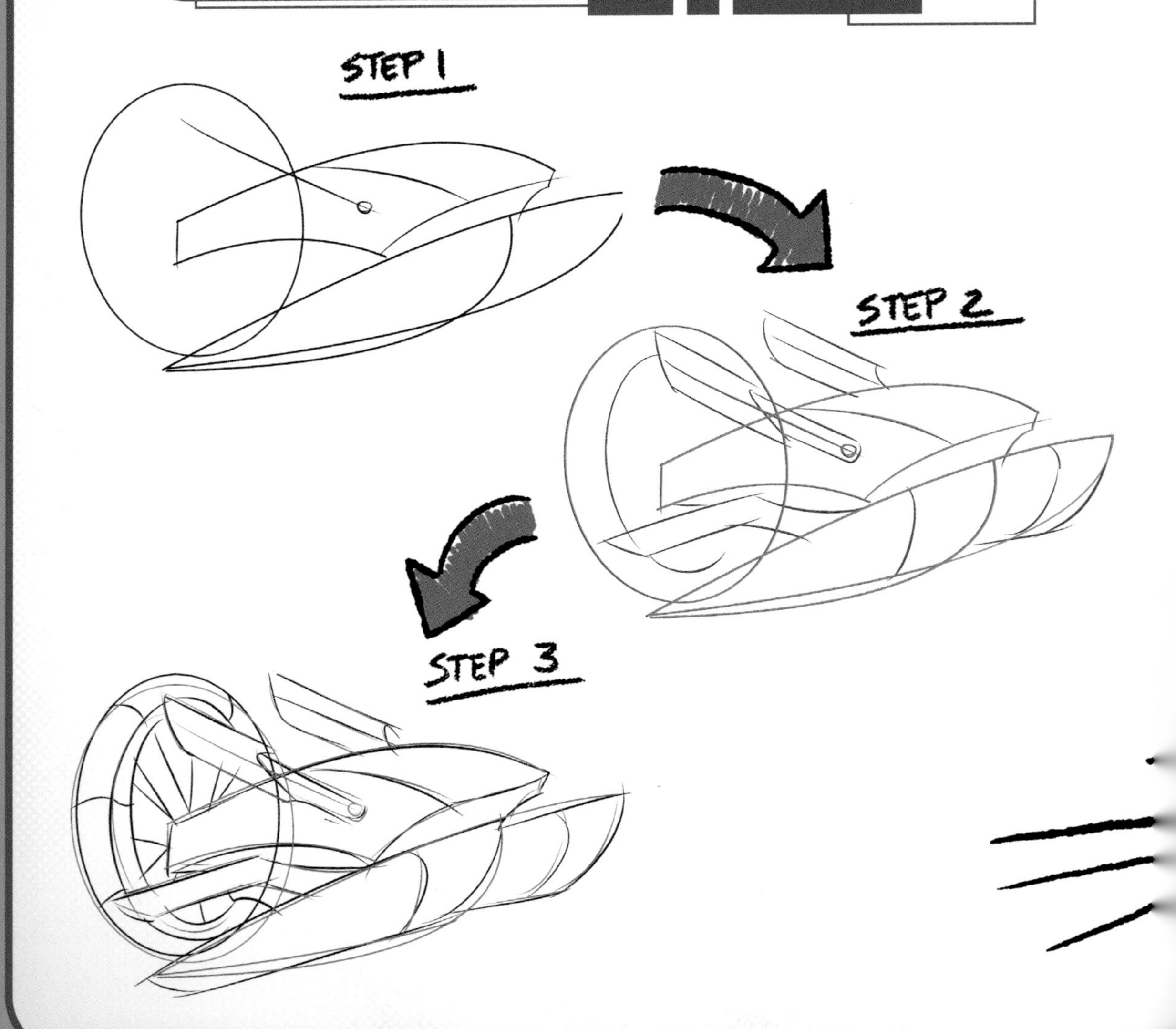

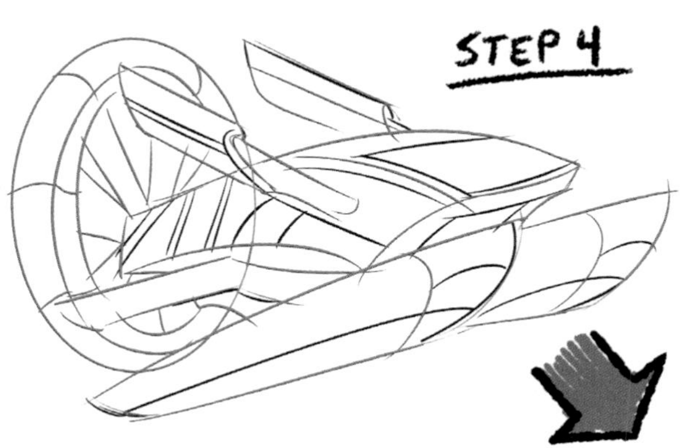

TIPS

Try adding different aquatic accessories. Maybe your ro-boat needs a bigger motor or a jet boost. Or go the opposite way and add a sail and rigging. How about a paddle wheel or some oars?

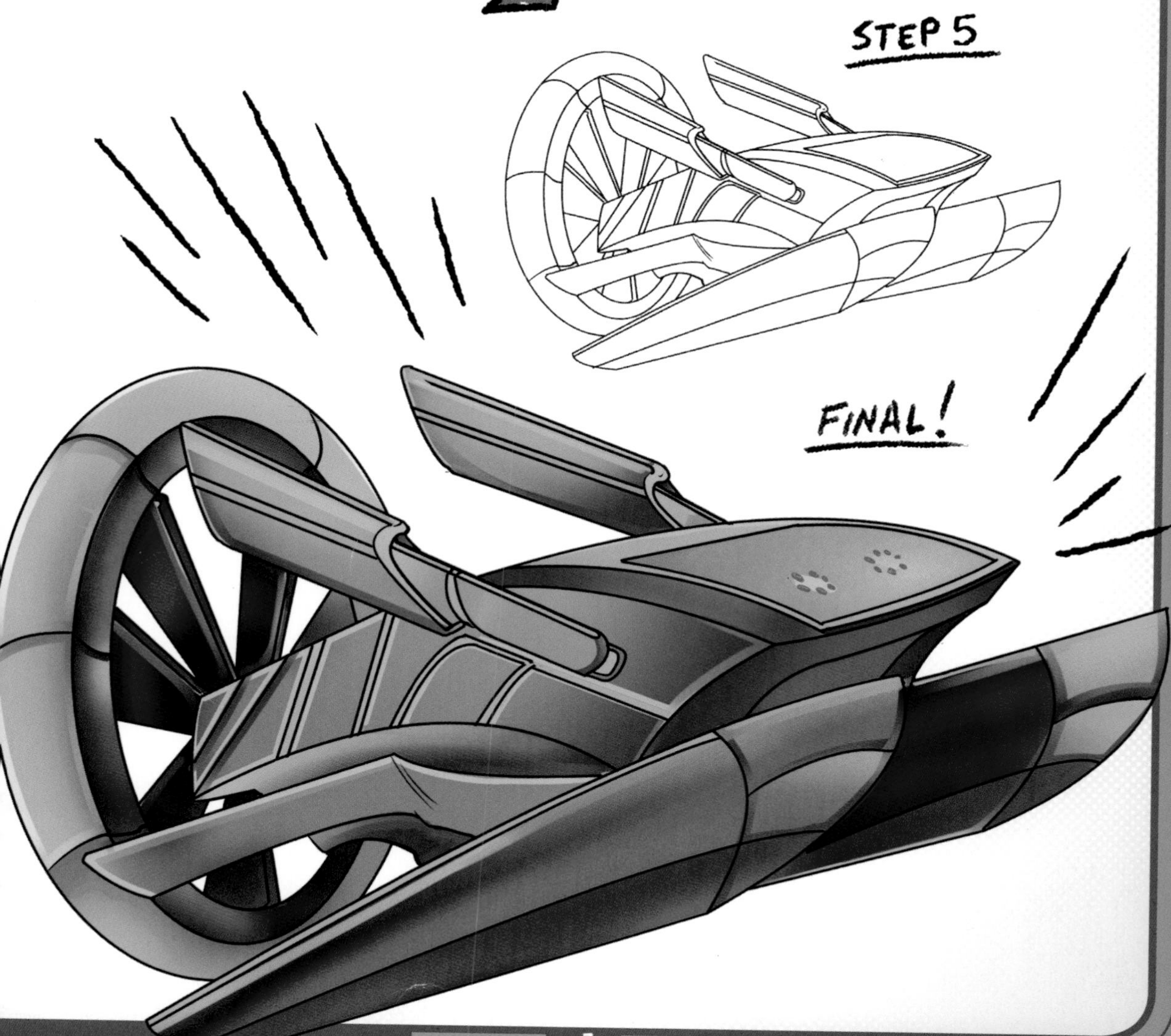

ROBO-CLIMBER

Reach new heights of exploration with a climber that never gets tired. It will swing, pick, and climb up the steepest peaks without fear.

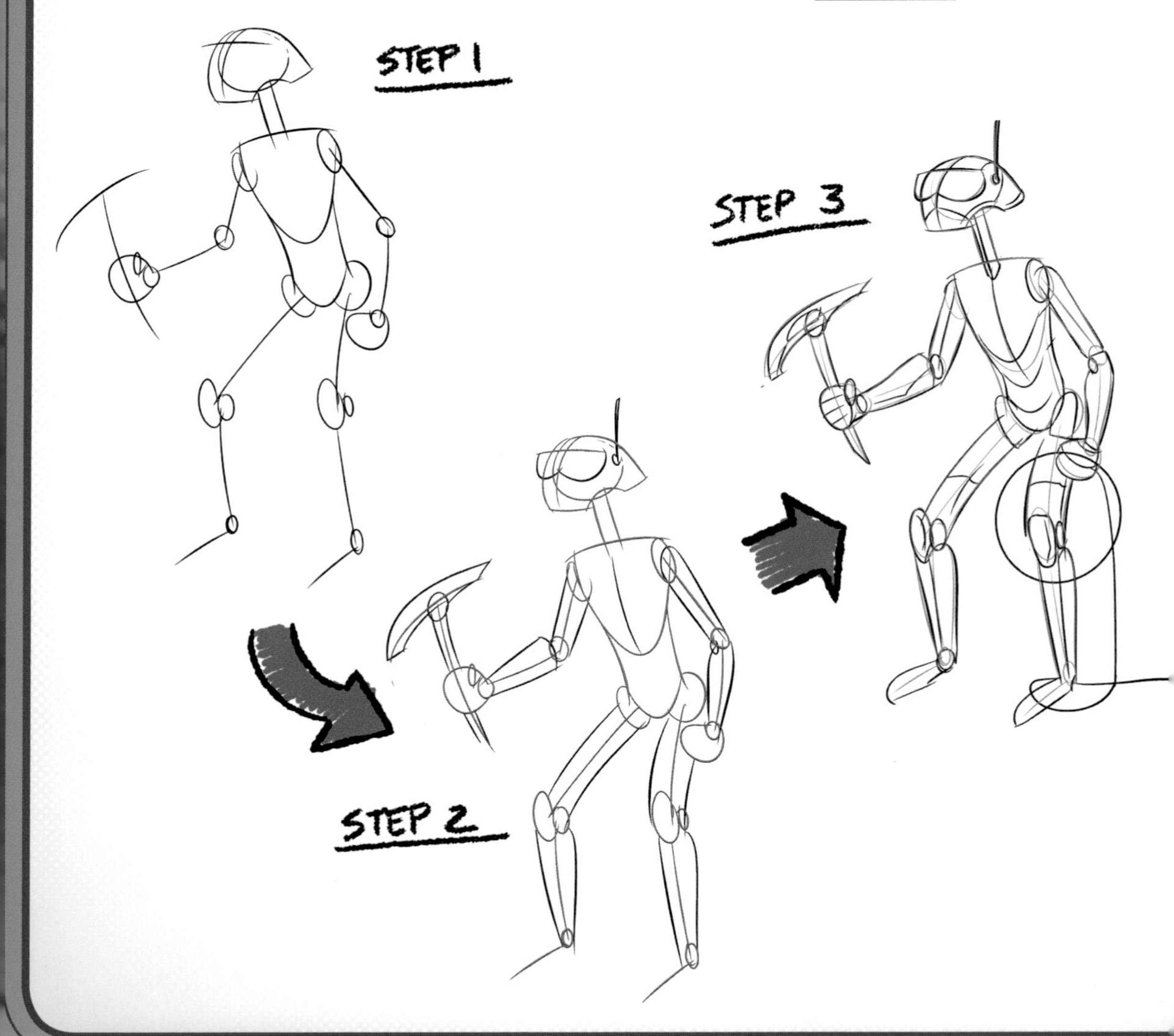

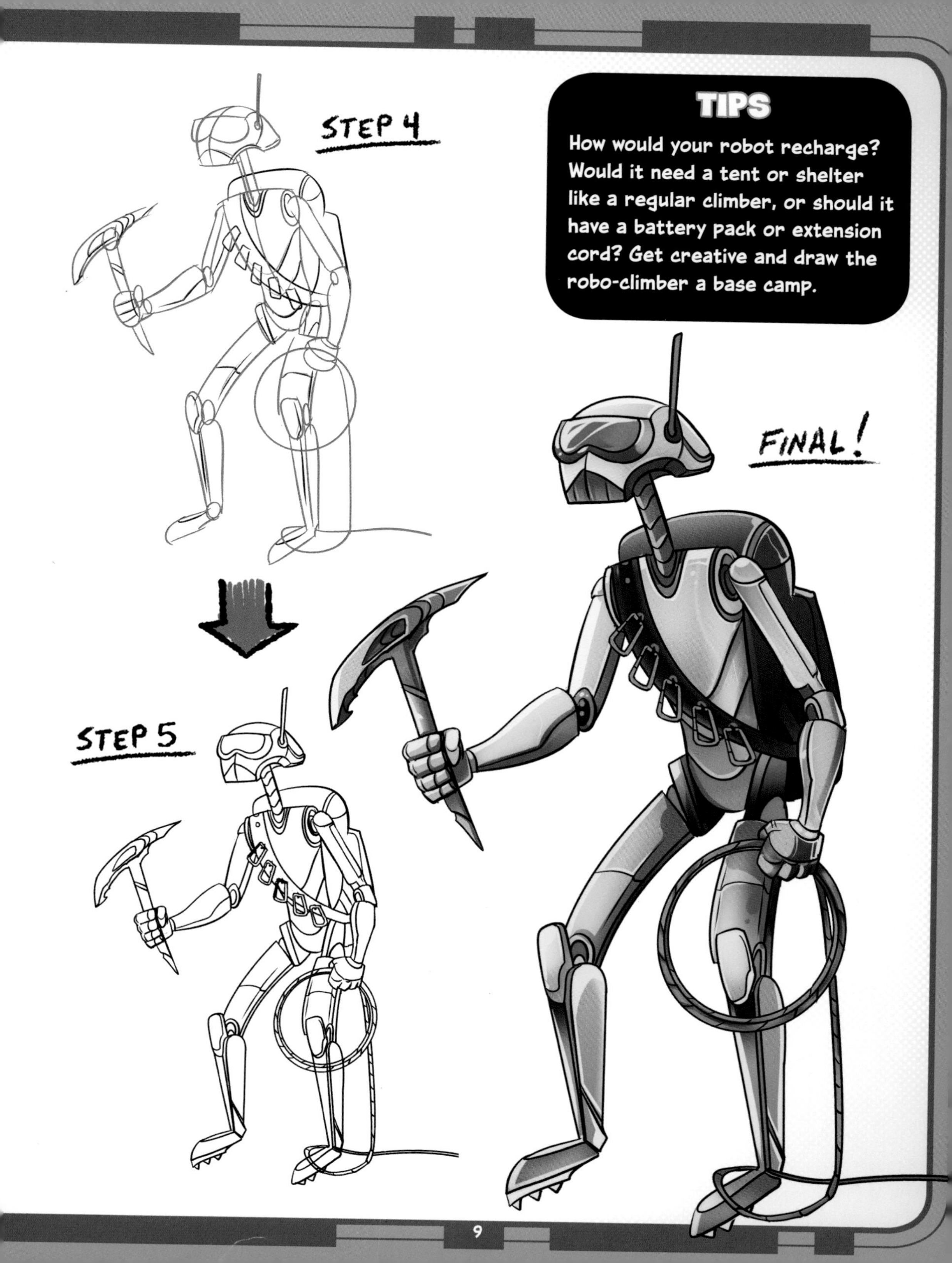
STEP 4
TIPS
How would your robot recharge? Would it need a tent or shelter like a regular climber, or should it have a battery pack or extension cord? Get creative and draw the robo-climber a base camp.
FINAL!
STEP 5

COWBOT OF THE OLD WEST

This cowbot may be the quickest draw in the west. With a sharp pencil and fresh pad of paper, you might be even faster. Care to challenge him?

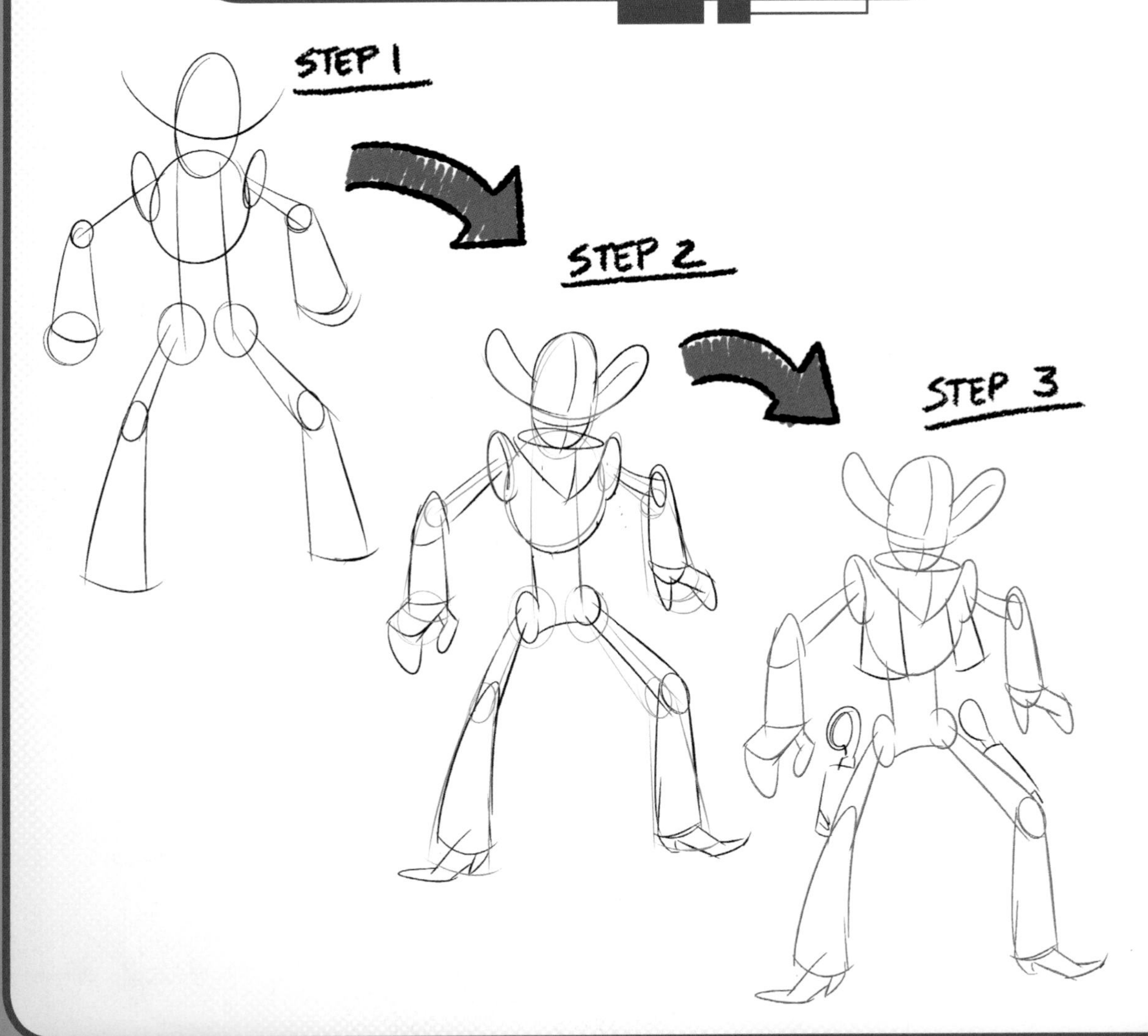

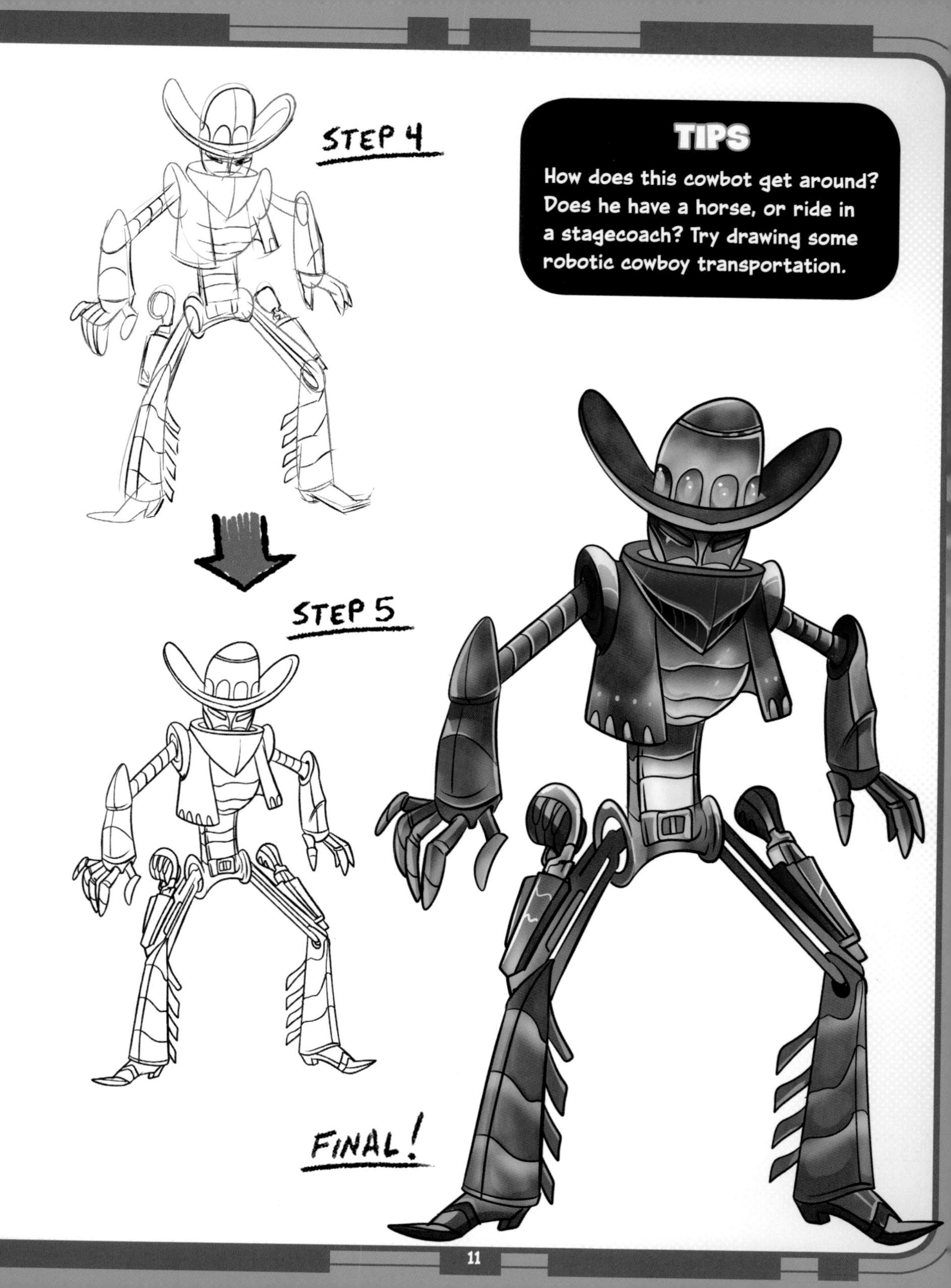
STEP 4
TIPS
How does this cowbot get around? Does he have a horse, or ride in a stagecoach? Try drawing some robotic cowboy transportation.
STEP 5
FINAL!

B-BOTS & B-GIRLS

No one can pop and lock like this b-bot dancer. It can master power moves and freezes like a pro. Plus, it provides its own beatbox!

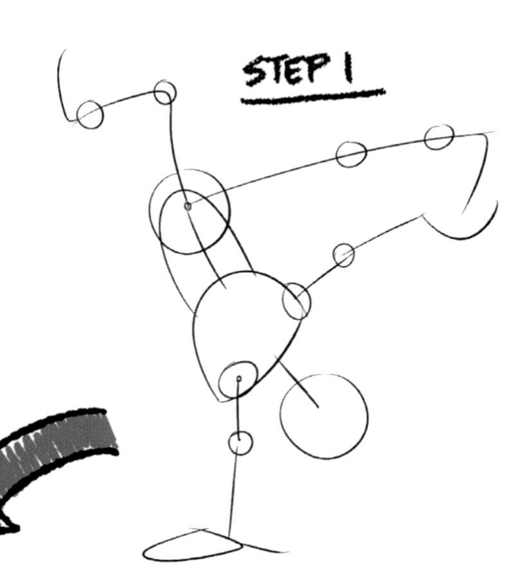

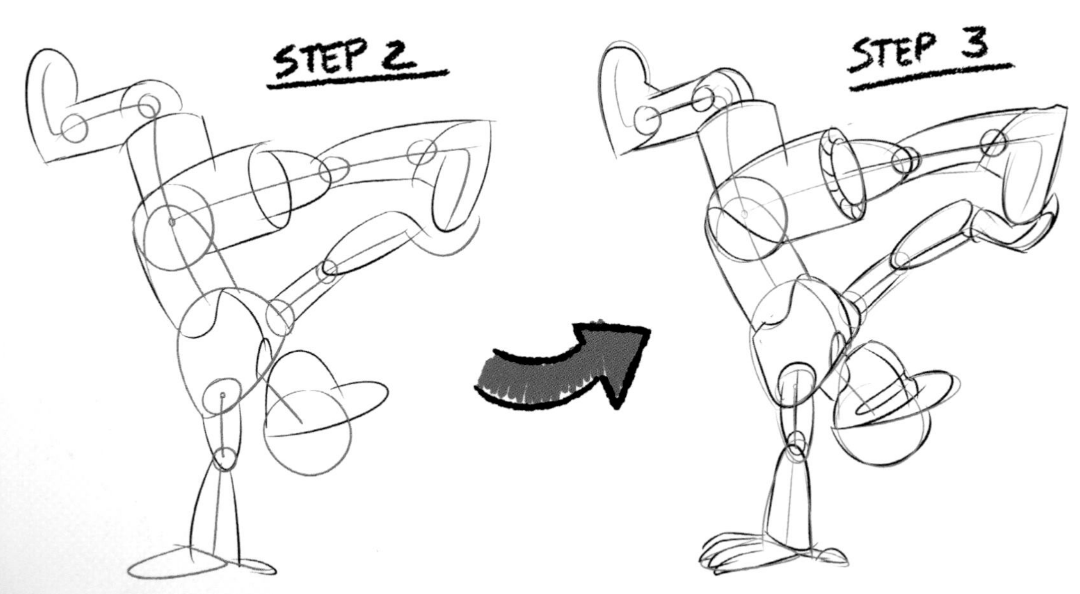

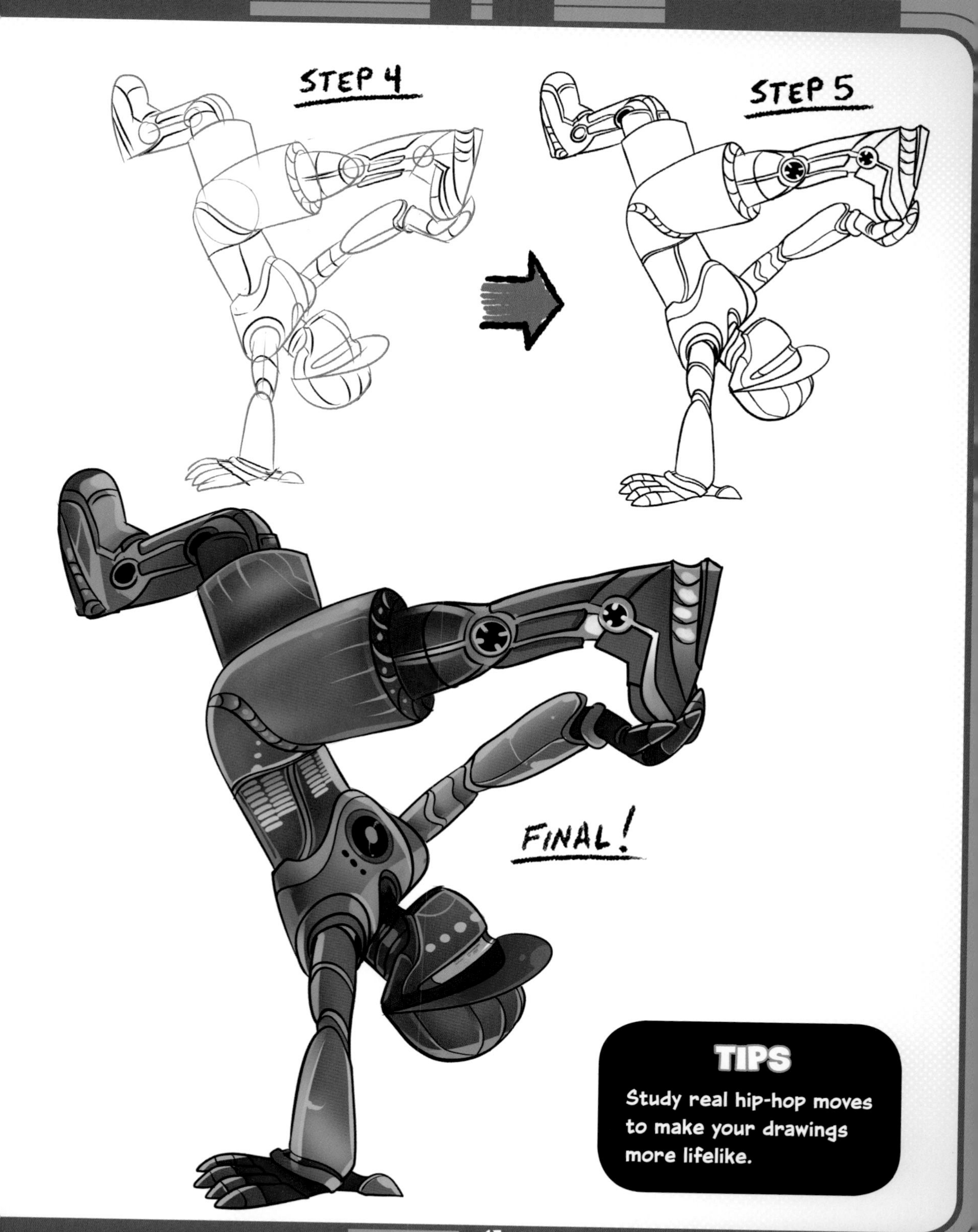

TIPS

Study real hip-hop moves to make your drawings more lifelike.

HEAVY METALS

Rescuing people from burning buildings is no big deal when you're fireproof! This robotic firefighter carries its own water supply, and breathing in smoke is never an issue. Just call for help and it'll be there in a flash.

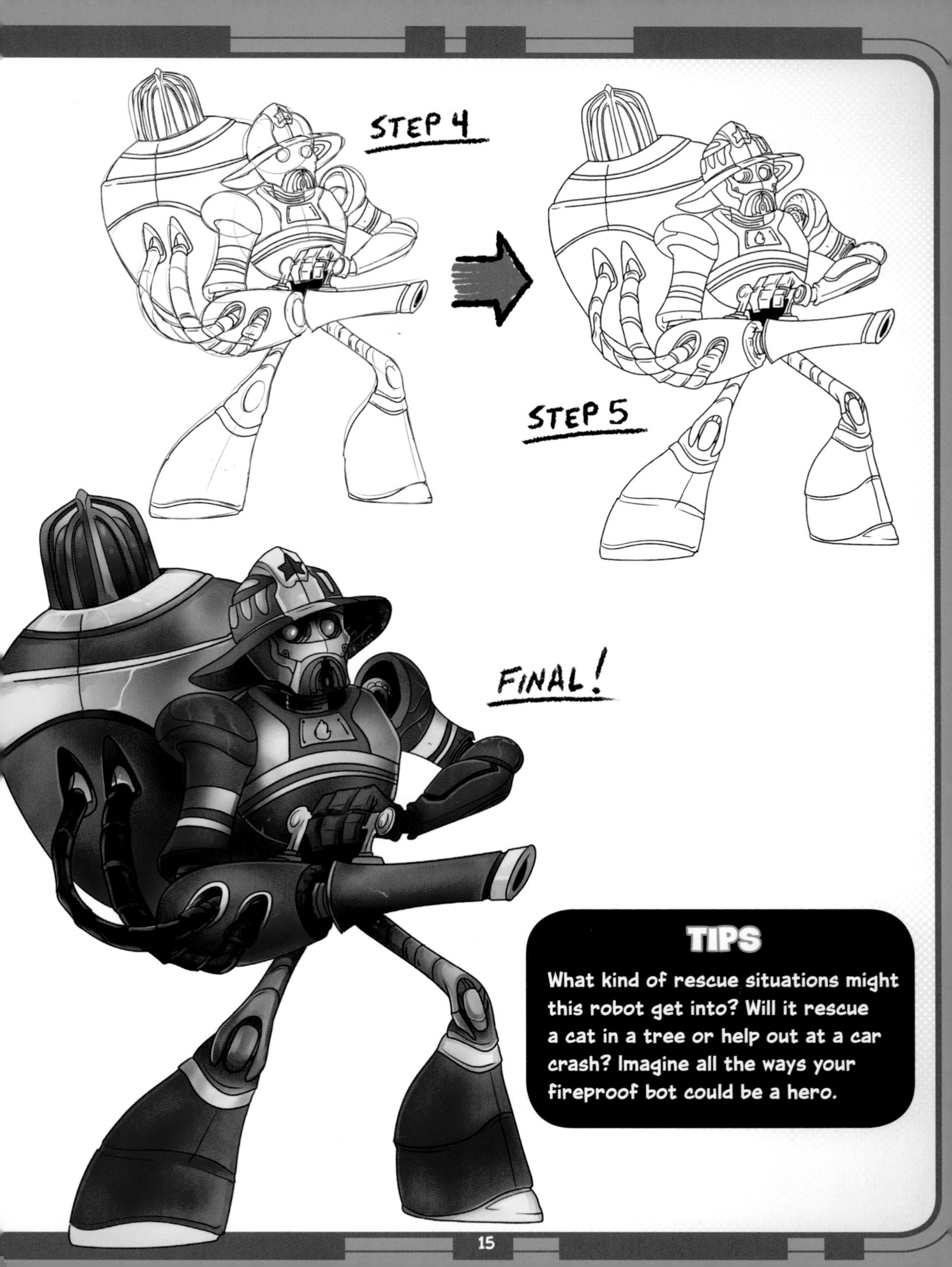

TIPS

What kind of rescue situations might this robot get into? Will it rescue a cat in a tree or help out at a car crash? Imagine all the ways your fireproof bot could be a hero.

FANTASY FOOTBALL MVP

This sporting robot has record-breaking passing yards, 100 percent accuracy, and never-ending energy. It's a fantasy football fan's most valuable player.

STEP 1

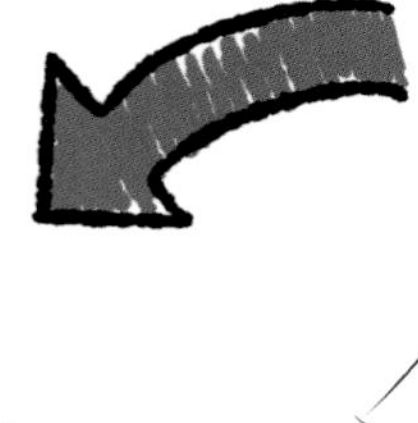

STEP 2

STEP 3

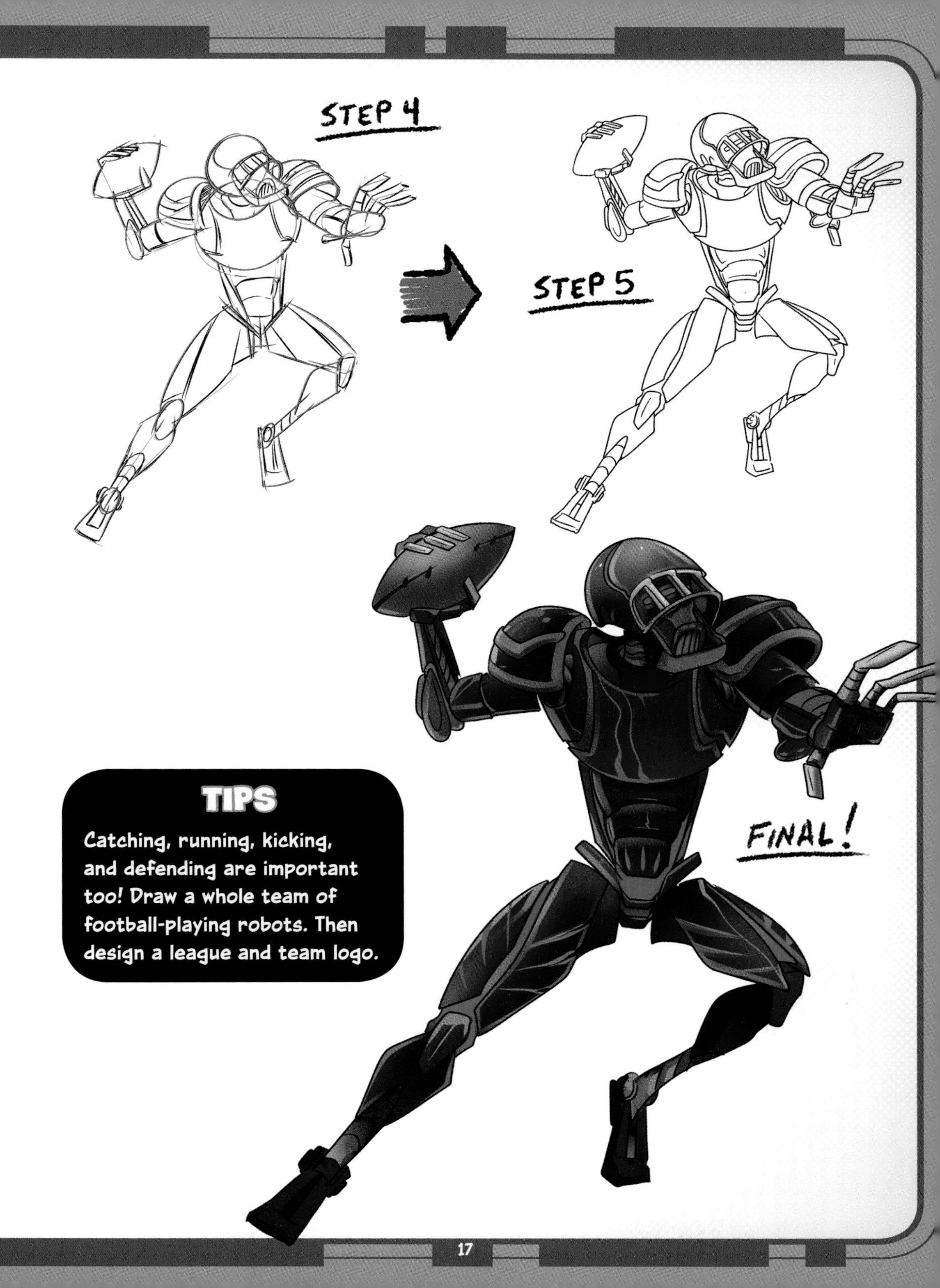

TIPS

Catching, running, kicking, and defending are important too! Draw a whole team of football-playing robots. Then design a league and team logo.

MAGICAL MACHINE

You can't help but admire the talents of this machine of misdirection! Programmed for amazing illusions, this magical machine is ready to dazzle the mind and awe the audience.

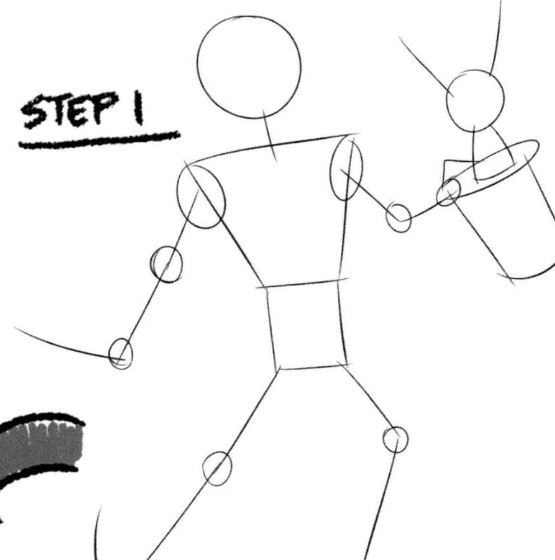

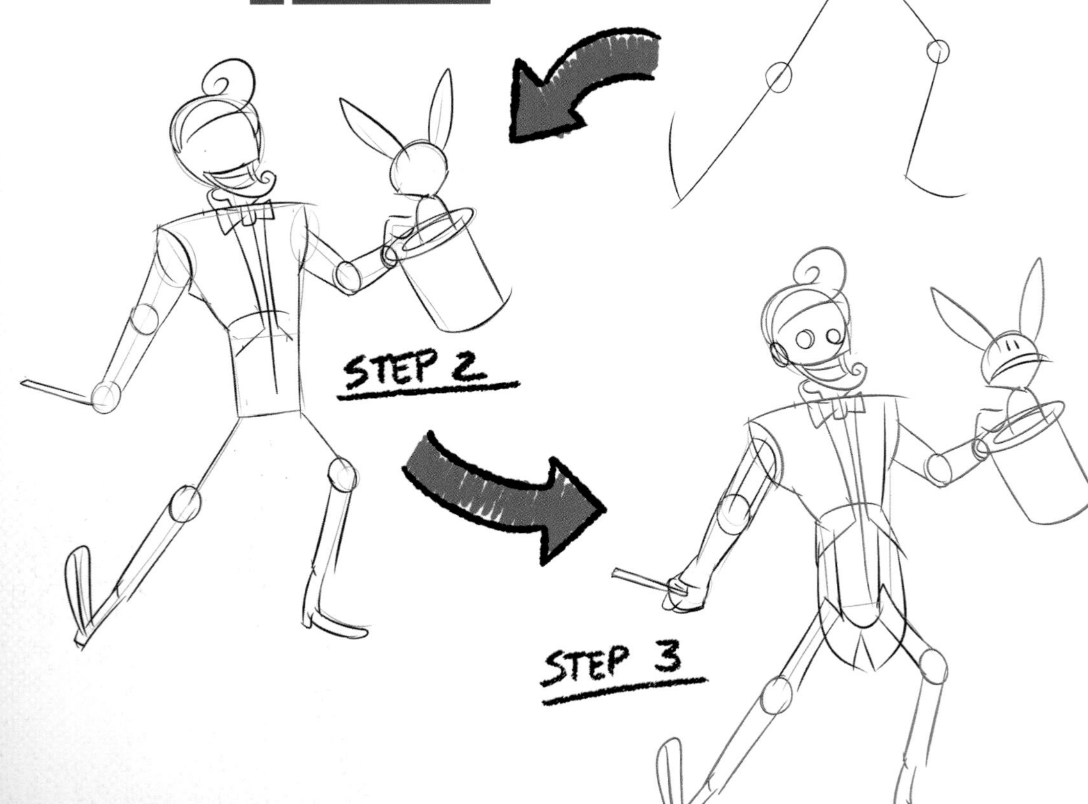

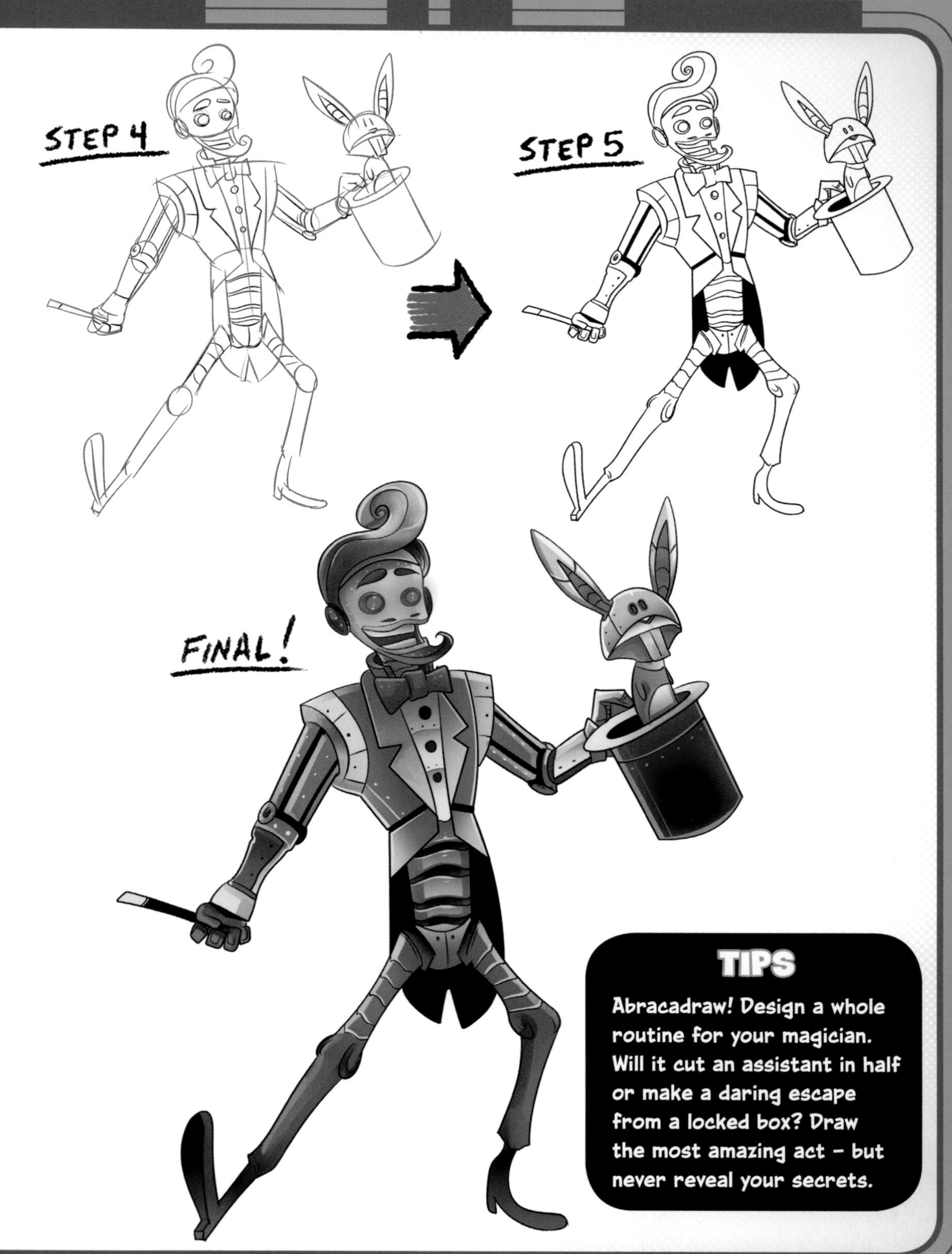

TIPS

Abracadraw! Design a whole routine for your magician. Will it cut an assistant in half or make a daring escape from a locked box? Draw the most amazing act – but never reveal your secrets.

DREAD PIRATE ROBOTS

Sail the high seas in a welded warship captained by Dread Pirate Robots. But hang onto your gold – the captain would rather have your extra nuts and bolts!

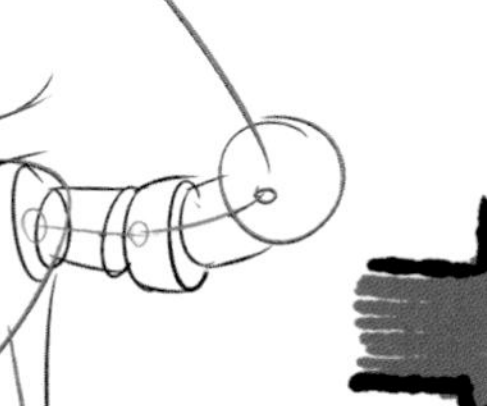

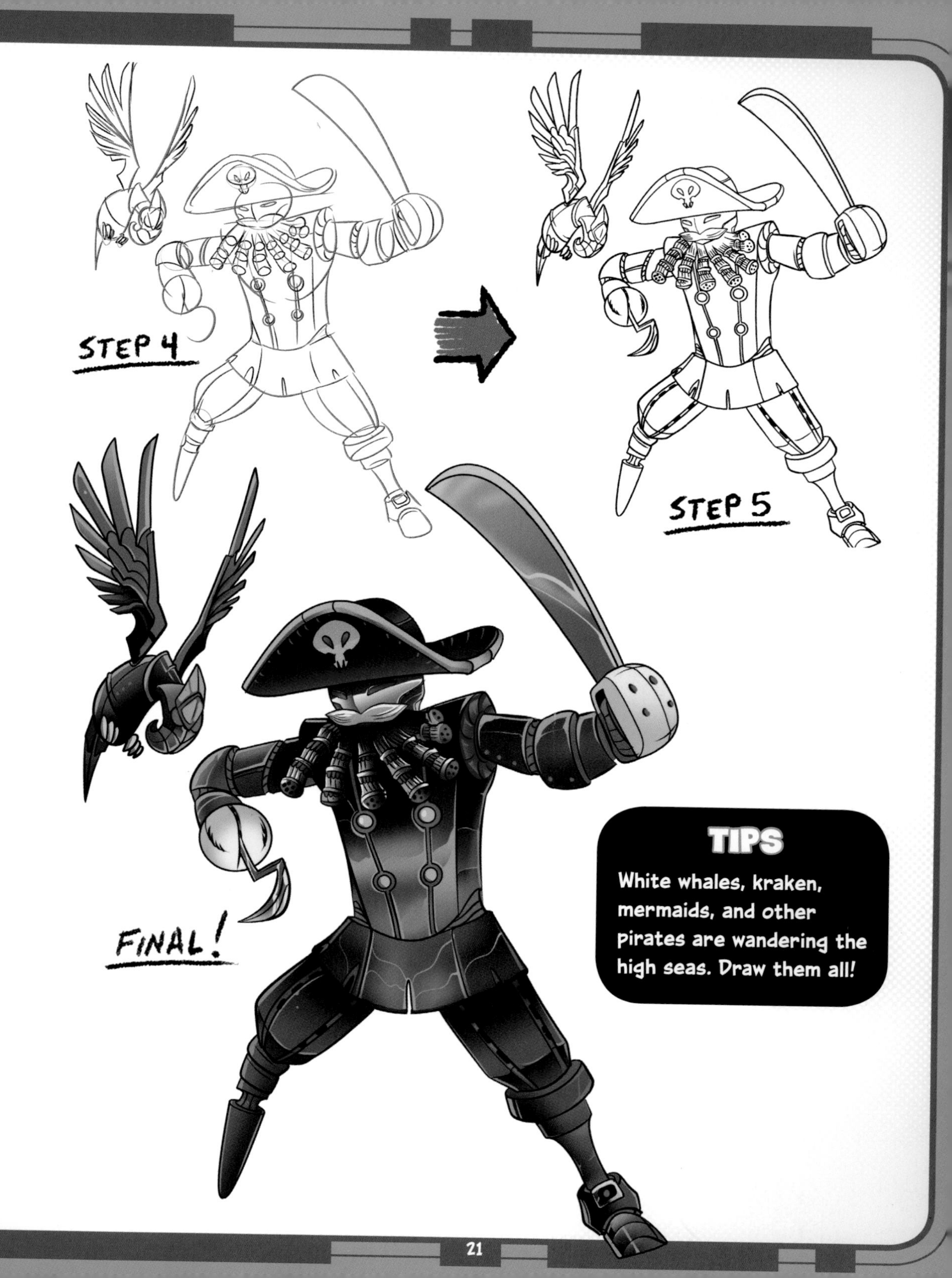
STEP 4
STEP 5
FINAL!
TIPS
White whales, kraken, mermaids, and other pirates are wandering the high seas. Draw them all!

RASCALLY RAB-BOT

Jackrabbits can run up to 45 miles (72 kilometers) per hour. This jacked-up rabbit is much faster!

STEP 1

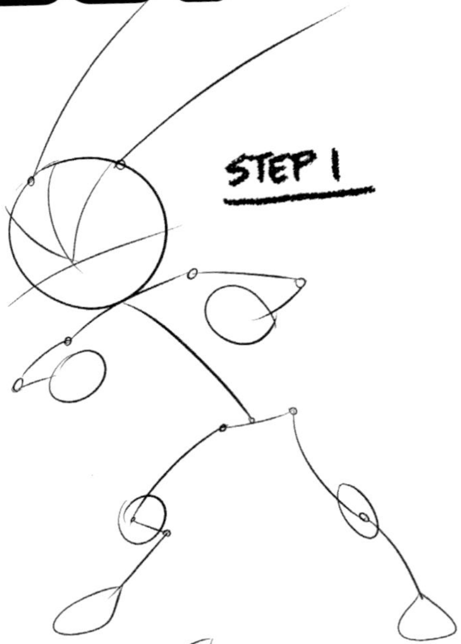

STEP 2

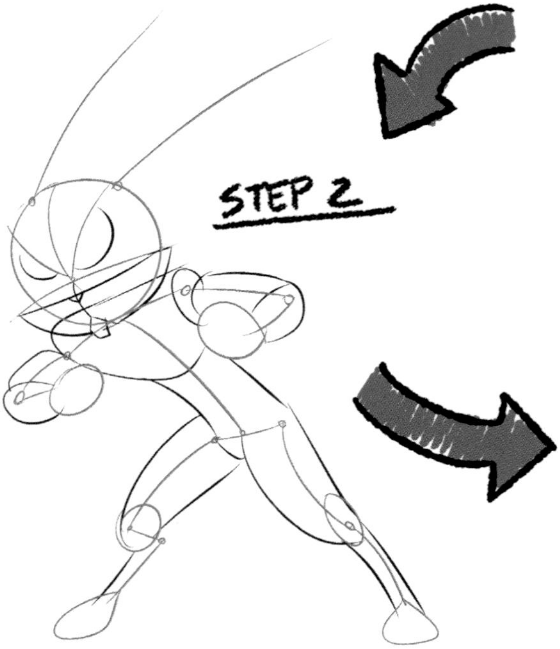

STEP 3

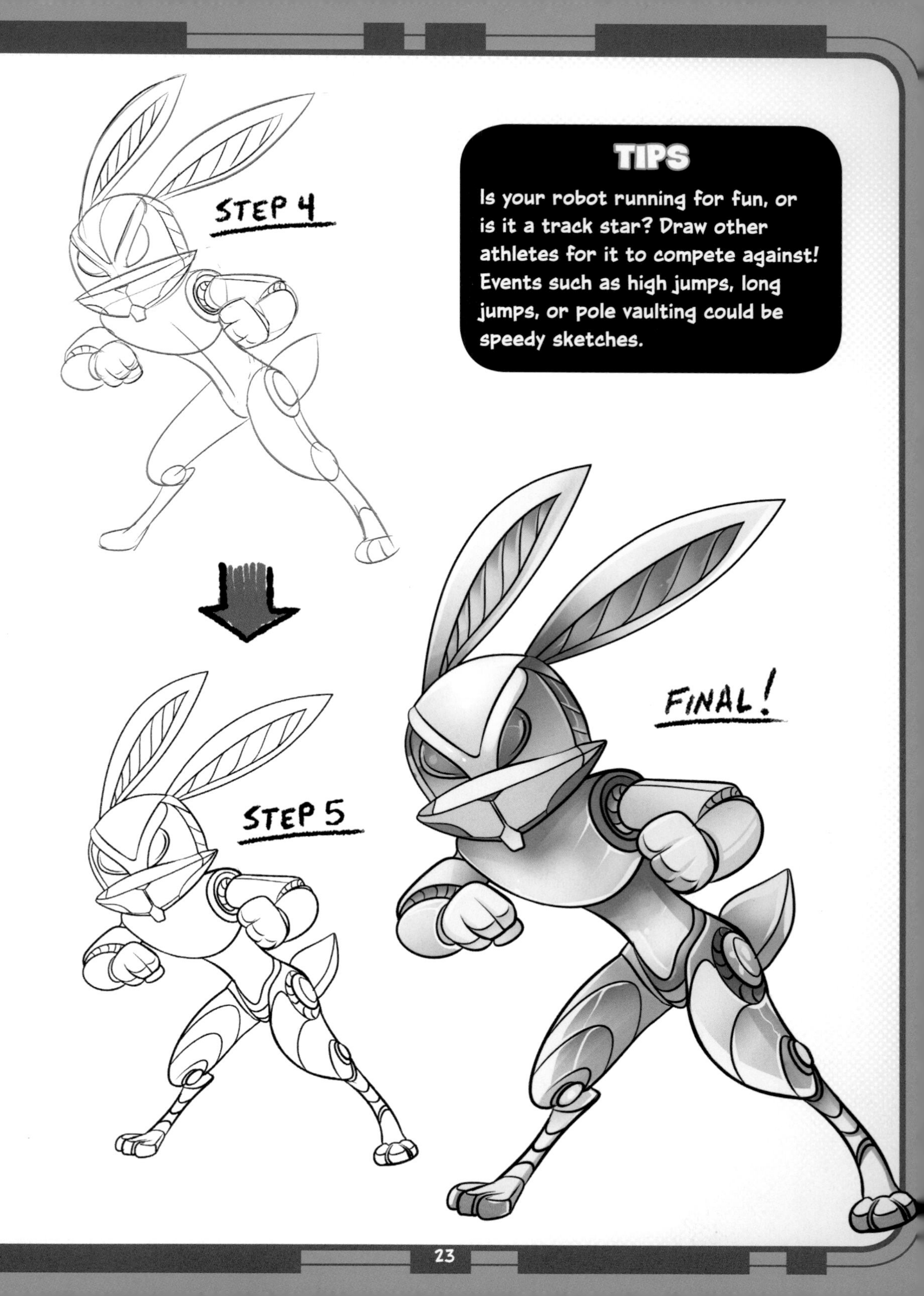
STEP 4
TIPS
Is your robot running for fun, or is it a track star? Draw other athletes for it to compete against! Events such as high jumps, long jumps, or pole vaulting could be speedy sketches.
STEP 5
FINAL!

SOLAR-POWERED SAMURAI

This samurai gets its powers from the sun's rays. That means it will never run out of energy, and can fight forever. Make sure this super soldier is on your side!

STEP 1

STEP 3

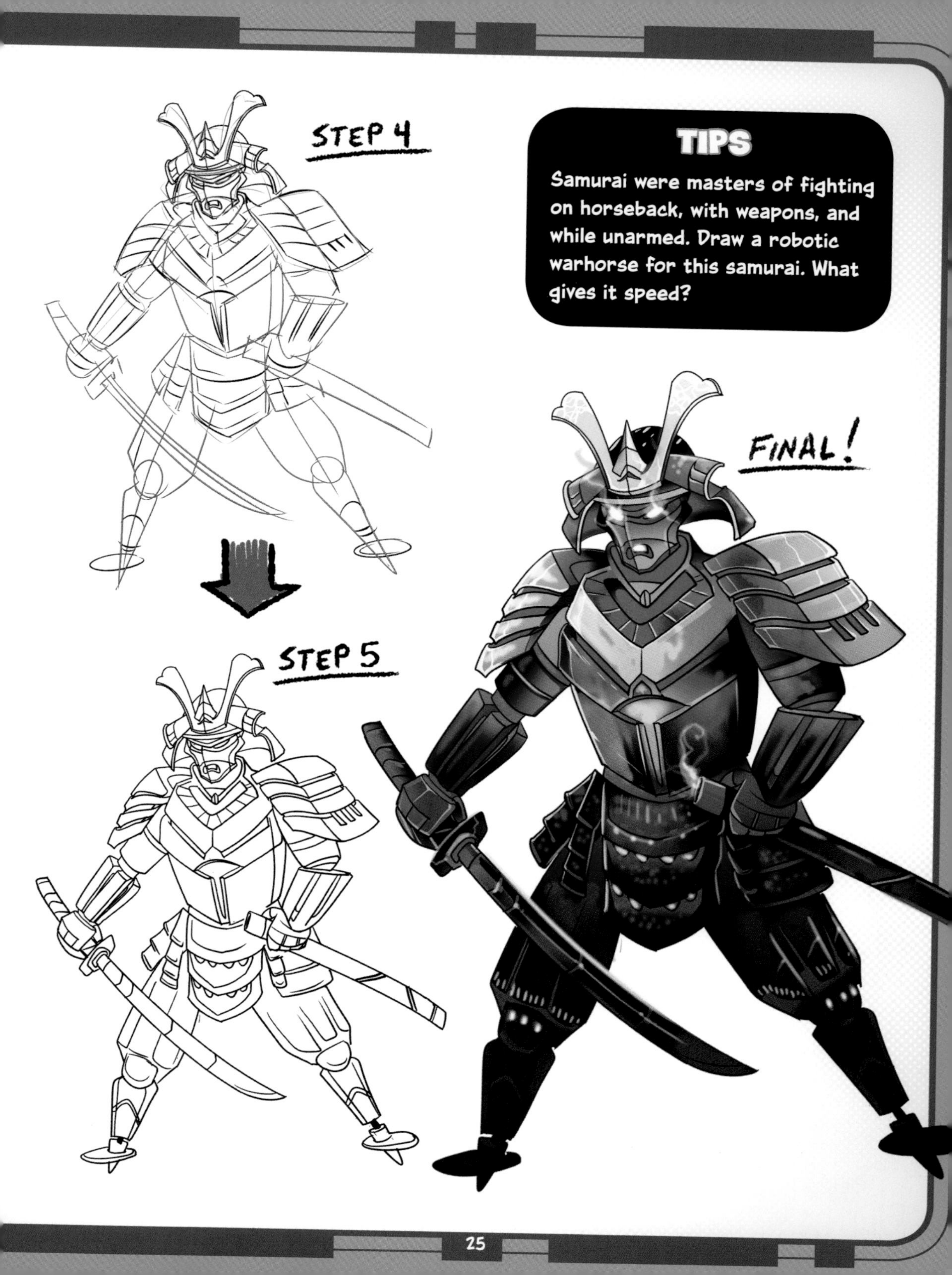

TIPS

Samurai were masters of fighting on horseback, with weapons, and while unarmed. Draw a robotic warhorse for this samurai. What gives it speed?

HIGH-SPEED SKATER

Speed skaters fly across the ice at speeds of 35 miles (56 km) per hour or more. Perfect balance and technology upgrades guarantee this bot has super speed.

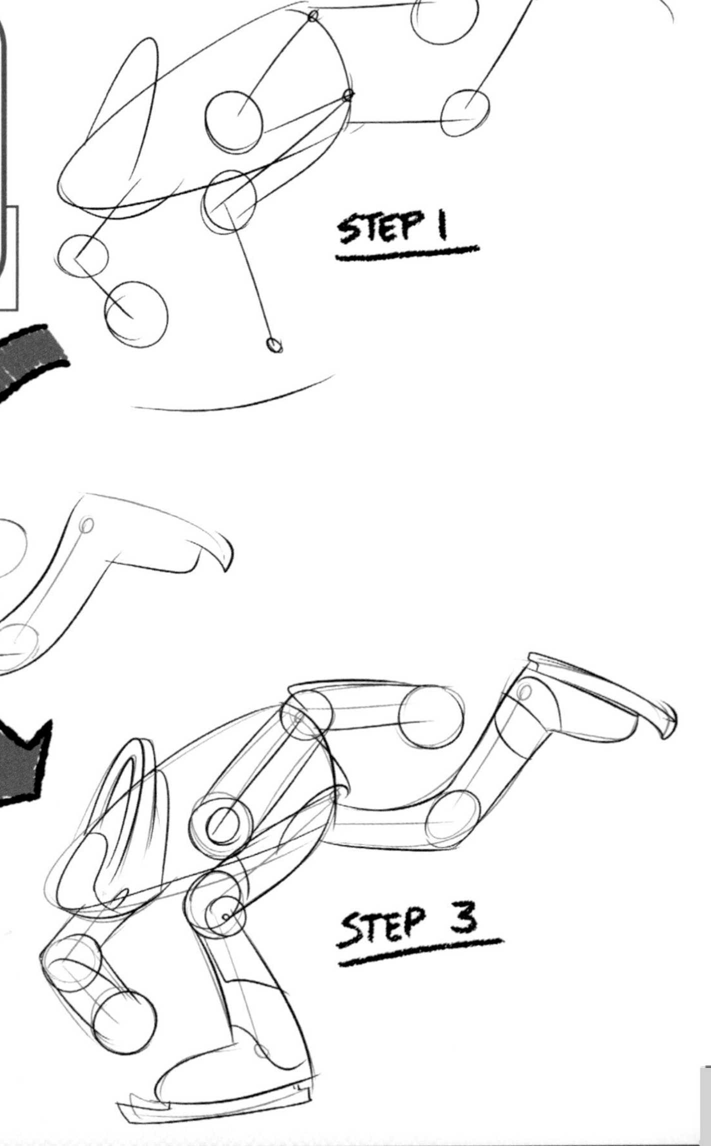

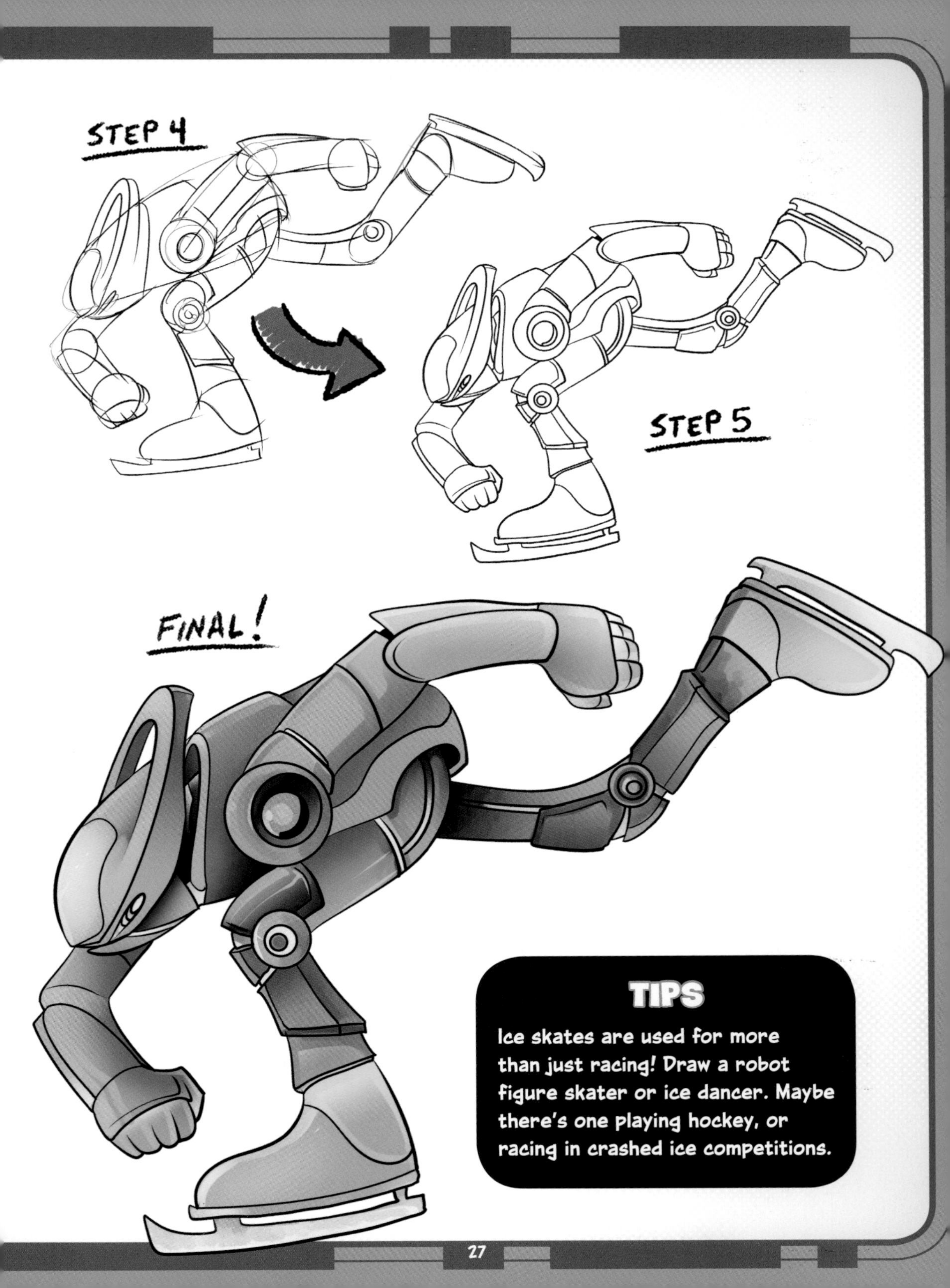

TIPS

Ice skates are used for more than just racing! Draw a robot figure skater or ice dancer. Maybe there's one playing hockey, or racing in crashed ice competitions.

EX-TERMINATOR

Good luck getting rid of this eight-legged mechanical monster! Once it's moved in to your home, it's there to stay.

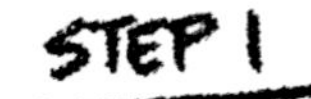

STEP 3

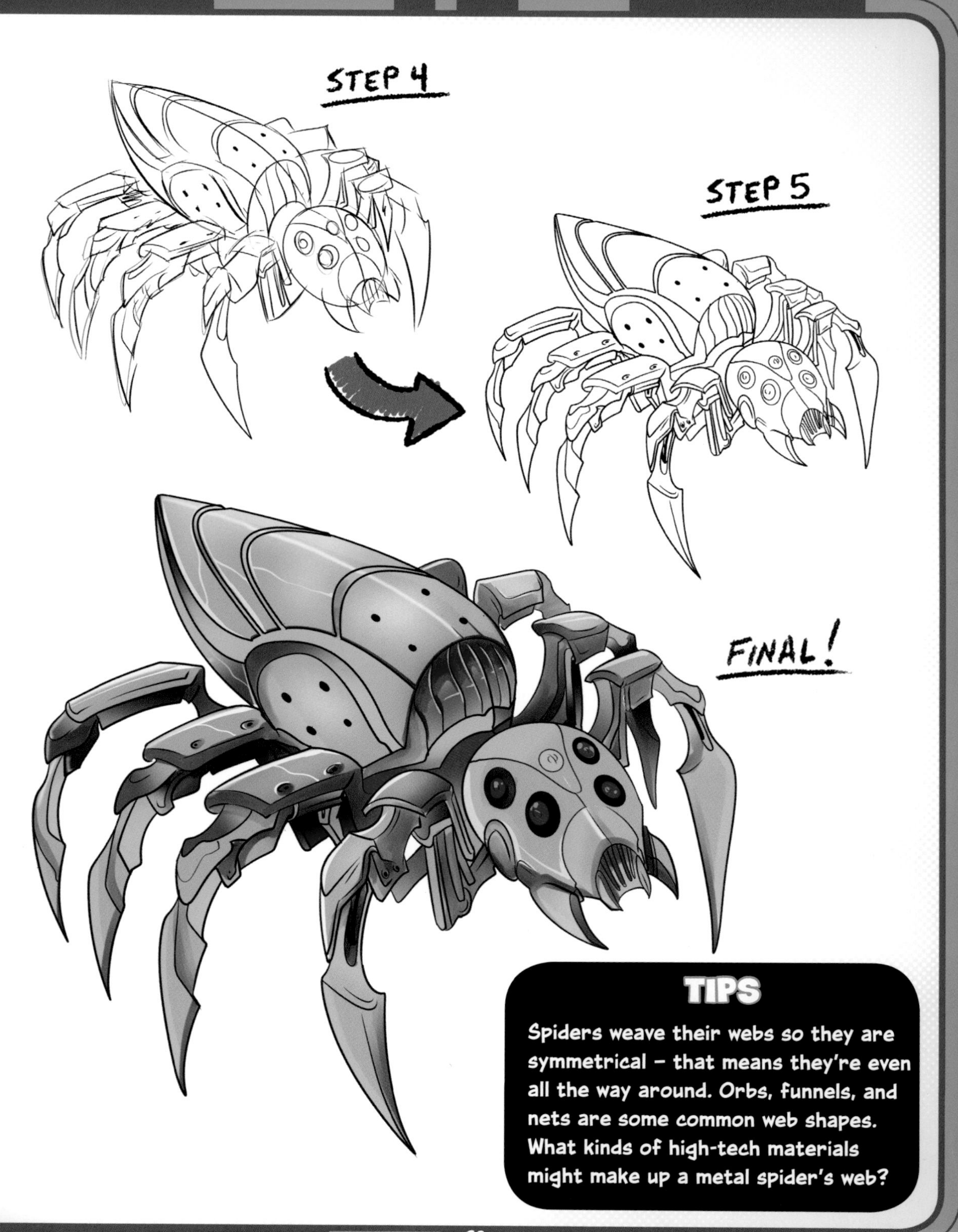

TIPS

Spiders weave their webs so they are symmetrical – that means they're even all the way around. Orbs, funnels, and nets are some common web shapes. What kinds of high-tech materials might make up a metal spider's web?

RECYLING
WITH A SMILE

This recycler is happy to head to work every day! Keeping the planet clean and tidy is what this handy bot lives for.

STEP 1

STEP 2

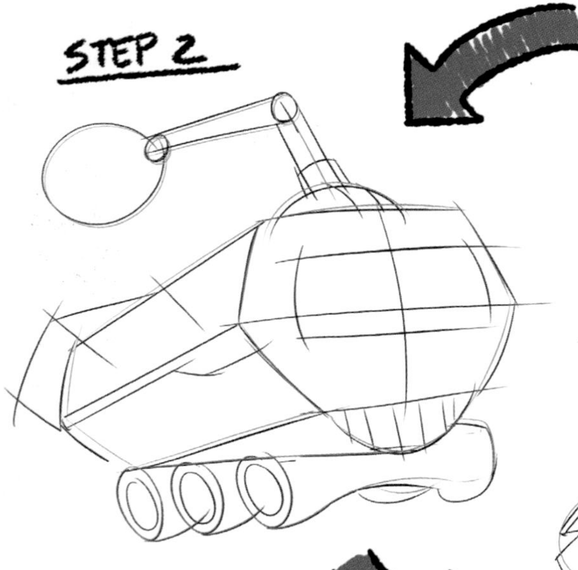

STEP 3

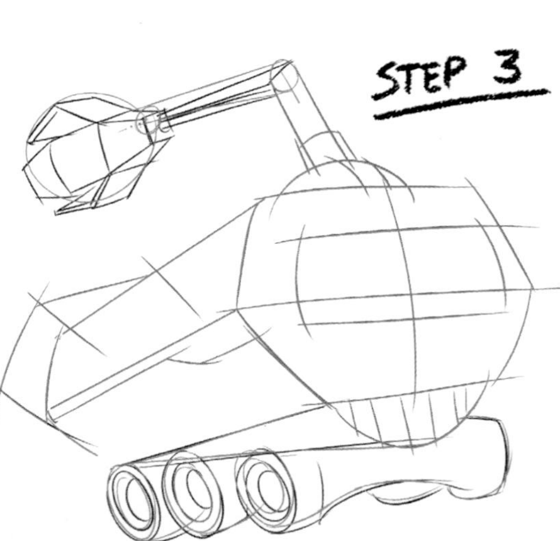

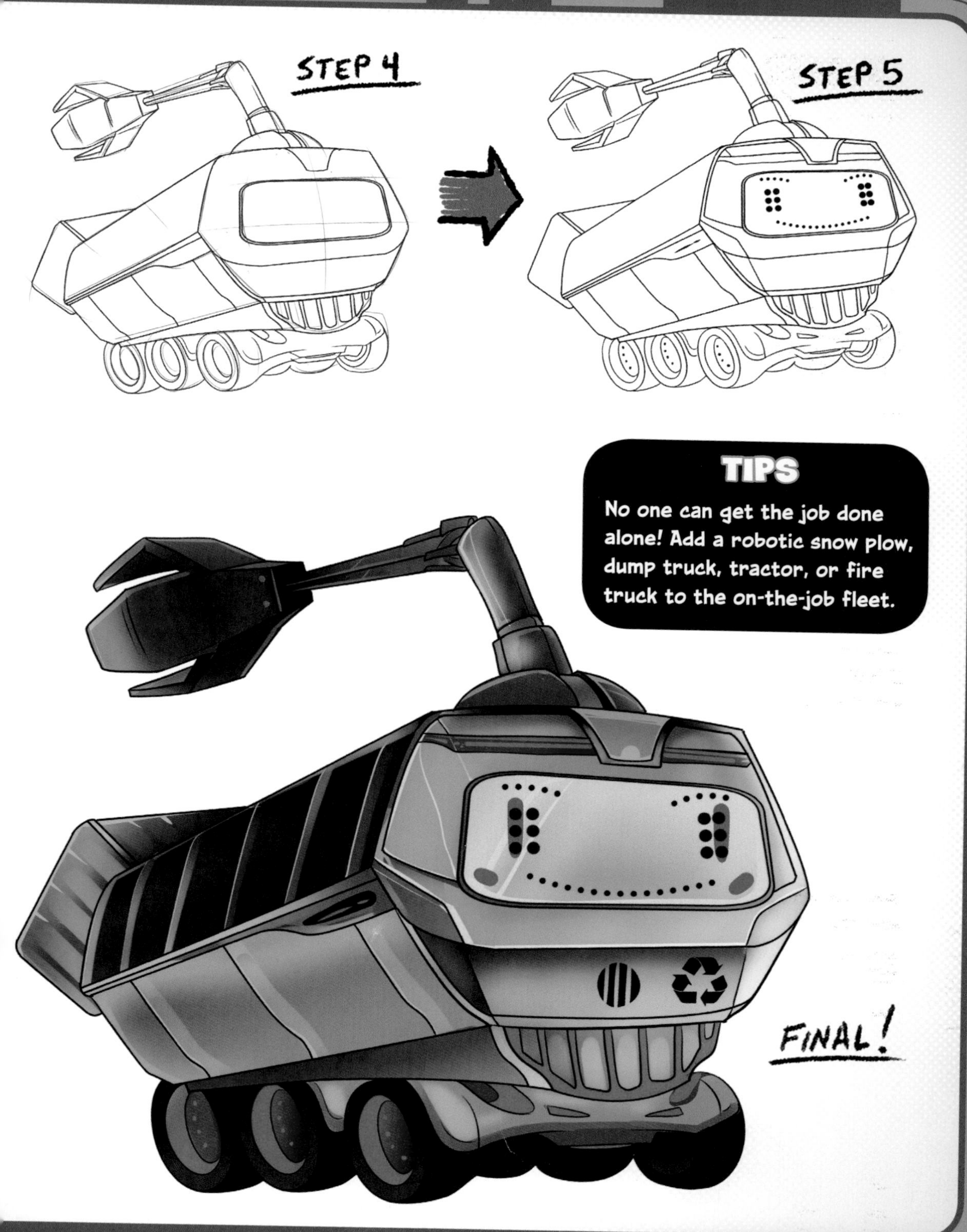
STEP 4
STEP 5
TIPS
No one can get the job done alone! Add a robotic snow plow, dump truck, tractor, or fire truck to the on-the-job fleet.
FINAL!

Read More

Bird, Benjamin. *Animal Doodles With Scooby-Doo!* North Mankato, Minn.: Capstone Press, 2017.

Gowen, Fiona. *How to Draw Scary Monsters and Other Mythical Creatures.* Hauppauge, N.Y.: Barrons Educational Series, 2017.

Young, Tim. *Creatures and Characters: Drawing Amazing Monsters, Aliens, and Other Weird Things!* Atglen, Penn.: Schiffer Pub., Ltd., 2017.

Internet Sites

Use FactHound to find Internet sites related to this book.

Visit *www.facthound.com*

Just type in 9781515769347 and go.